Praise f

THE AL.

Whistler Independent Book Awards 2022
GOLD MEDAL WINNER
- Category Children.

Reader's Favorite Book Awards 2021
GOLD MEDAL WINNER
- Category Preteen.

Wishing Shelf Book Awards 2019-2020
SILVER MEDAL WINNER
- Category Teenagers.

Feathered Quill Book Awards 2021
FINALIST
- Category Young Readers.

IAN Book of the Year Awards 2020
FINALIST
- Category Juvenile.

Reviews:

"An extremely timely message for today's readers."

"Solid aliens-crash-to-earth tale."

"The author has buckets and buckets of imagination."

"The entire series is absolutely fantastic!"

BOOKS BY RAE KNIGHTLY

The Great War of the Kins - Prequel
Subscribe at: www.raeknightly.com

THE ALIEN SKILL SERIES

Ben Archer and the Cosmic Fall, Book 1
https://www.amazon.com/dp/1989605192

Ben Archer and the Alien Skill, Book 2
https://www.amazon.com/dp/1989605095

Ben Archer and the Moon Paradox, Book 3
https://www.amazon.com/dp/1989605141

Ben Archer and the World Beyond, Book 4
https://www.amazon.com/dp/1989605044

Ben Archer and the Star Rider, Book 5
https://www.amazon.com/dp/1989605176

Ben Archer and the Toreq Son, Book 6
https://www.amazon.com/dp/1989605214

THE LOST SPACE TREASURE SERIES

The Lost Space Treasure – A Novella
https://www.amazon.com/dp/B0BKFXY87S

Exostar, Book 1
https://www.amazon.com/dp/B0BKFYBP4V

The Knowledge Seeker
https://www.amazon.com/dp/1989605311

THE
LOST
SPACE
TREASURE

A NOVELLA

Rae Knightly

THE LOST SPACE TREASURE, A NOVELLA
Copyright © 2022 by Rae Knightly.

For information, go to:
www.raeknightly.com

Cover design by PINTADO
Book Formatting by Derek Murphy @Creativindie
Published by PoCo Publishers
ISBN Paperback: 978-1-989605-46-2

First Edition: November 2022

For you, who will set foot on Mars.

CONTENTS

THE LOST SPACE TREASURE - SPACE MAP

NUMEN

ALLUVIUM

MAGNUS STAR CLUSTER

ORBITUS

INTERSTELLAR ALLIANCE

PLETHORA

CIVICUS-1
CIVICUS-2
CIVICUS-3

ENILLON

THYPSO

GALLIVANTO

GEMELO

EXHIBITUS

KEPRA-1
KEPRA-2

LLUUNIDES

VUNKOTUNE

© Rae Knightly

EXHIBITUS
ARTIFICIAL MOON ORBITING THE
WANDERING PLANET, GALLIVANTO,
MAGNUS STAR CLUSTER,
MILKY WAY GALAXY.
INTEREST: POLITICAL AND CULTURAL CENTER
OF THE INTERSTELLAR ALLIANCE.

CHAPTER 1 *Robot Teacher*

The android turned and smiled at the students. A static line scrolled up its screen, briefly distorting the image of its pleasant face. "Quiet down, class," the artificial teacher said, raising a metal finger to its pixelated lips.

A ripple of excitement traveled through the middle graders as they commented on the bold 3-D letters projected above the entrance to the high-tech museum.

The letters read:

EXHIBITUS MUSEUM
Heart of the
INTERSTELLAR ALLIANCE

Welcome to the
PROF. NANDO PAZORRI EXHIBITION;
Citizen of Enillon,
Space explorer,
Anthropologist,
Adventurer,
Hero.
Discoverer of the EXOSTAR.

Enter the world of the legendary
LOST SPACE TREASURE.

Before the entrance to the museum, a massive statue of a young man in space attire, pointing with his right arm into the distance, dwarfed the students.

"He's so handsome!" girls quipped to each other, while boys narrowed their eyes and puffed out their chest to copy the thoughtful stance of the famous explorer.

It took a while before Ms. PT-A's class calmed down enough for her to speak again. "I know you are impatient to start exploring, but first, we must go over some important rules... KARAL! Leave Olivia's backpack alone!"

Twenty pairs of eyes turned to the student standing at the back of the group.

"Hey! That's mine! Give it back!" Olivia yelled, pulling at the strap of her backpack that stuck out of Karal's mouth.

Eight eyes sitting atop stalks on Karal's head blinked at her.

"Karal," Ms. PT-A scolded in a monotone voice, "We have been over this. I know you come from Lluunides and that you do things differently there, but you are old enough to know that—on the other Alliance planets—eating your companion's belongings is very rude. Now let go of the backpack or you will spend the rest of the day in the IQURUS, where you will wait for us to return from the exhibition!"

The strap slipped out of Karal's mouth.

"Good boy," Ms. PT-A praised. The teacher's hovering body spun toward the rest of the students with a soft buzz. "Class, remember to help your new companion. Moving to a different planet is difficult and takes a lot of adjustment. Now, where was I? Ah! Rules. We are ready to enter the Professor Nando Pazorri Exhibition..."

"I want to see the Exostar!" a girl complained, twirling a strand of hair around her finger while she chewed on a piece of gum.

"All in good time..."

"I want a hoverchair," a boy grumbled. "I'm *tired*."

"No, Thapu," the robot said evenly. "We will not get hoverchairs. Legs that are made of flesh and bone like yours, need exercise. I won't have laziness in my class. You will *walk* around the explorer's exhibition and I will hear no more of that hoverchair nonsense.

"You are free to wander on your own for two hours. I expect you to pay close attention to the information provided in this interactive exhibition. At the end of the tour, you will answer the ten questions that I am sending to your Mass Transfer devices now."

The children's ear devices pinged in unison at the incoming homework. Some students groaned while others stepped forward, eager to start the challenge.

"Wait." Ms. PT-A's four arms snapped out of her metal body to form a barrier. She turned up the volume of her voice to speak over the ruckus. "Listen, now! If you get lost in the forest, stung by a venomous arachnis or eaten by cannibals, please proceed to the EXIT sign blinking on your MT map, located at the end of the main hall. We will regroup there for lunch before we visit the Exostar."

Cheers exploded throughout the group, making some well-dressed alien visitors arriving at the intergalactic museum glance at them with a frown.

Ms. PT-A's outstretched arms reintegrated into her metallic frame and the students broke into a run. They crossed the spacious terrace leading to the exhibition and were soon swallowed up into a virtual universe filled with danger and wonder.

Ms. PT-A smiled placidly and waved a mechanical hand after them. "Have fun, children."

CHAPTER 2 *The Space Explorer*

No sooner had the youngsters entered the museum than they were thrust into a virtual representation of the planet Enillon. They beamed with pride at seeing their home planet represented from the start of the tour.

They had traveled 5.2 light years from Enillon to Exhibitus yesterday by means of a government Interplanetary Quantum Rocket of Universal Standard—or *IQURUS*, as they were known. Indeed, a trip to the Exhibitus Museum was an obligatory outing in the school curriculum for all students belonging to the planets of the Interstellar Alliance.

"Welcome to the Professor Nando Pazorri Exhibition," a gentle museum-voice oozed into their earpiece. "We find ourselves at the beginning of our journey: the birthplace of the famous explorer.

"Born on the planet Enillon two hundred years before the rise of the Interstellar Alliance, young Nando grew up in a comfortable home on the grounds of the illustrious Pazorri University. His mother, Maria Pazorri—acclaimed historian of the A'hmun civilization and founder of the university—and his father, Ronaldo Russ—housefather—took great interest in their son's upbringing. Throughout his childhood, Nando was surrounded with books and scholars, and both fed his enormous curiosity of our universe."

Olivia adjusted her backpack on her shoulder and whispered into her MT device, "Question one: Professor Nando Pazorri was born two hundred years before the rise of the Interstellar Alliance." The device pinged in her ear as it logged her answer. She eyed Thapu, who stared with disinterest at the university's grand buildings and lush gardens. He had completely missed the answer to the first question.

Other students strolled away into neighboring virtual bubbles, grumbling at how boring it was to listen to background information. They wanted to get to the heart of the action!

Several agonizingly slow minutes passed while the museum-voice led the more patient students along the Professor's life trajectory: his excellent grades, his intelligent friends, his first discoveries of previously unknown worlds, and his ground-breaking archeological finds which could now be admired at the museum.

"Of course, Professor Pazorri is most well-known for his discovery of the Exostar and the legend of The Lost Space Treasure," the well-oiled museum-voice explained as it directed a handful of youngsters from one virtual set to another.

Olivia and Thapu ended up heading in the same direction, and they chatted excitedly at the prospect of nearing the famous diamond.

"Hold on a minute," Thapu whispered suddenly, pulling her back and pointing down. "Karal just came by here."

The alien child from Lluunides, who was sliding away to their left, had no legs or feet but, instead, had a long tail with six suckers in a hexagonal shape at its end. His slimy body left a wet trail behind him, forcing a diligent museum-robot to mop up the floor after him.

The two students stepped over the slippery section, sticking out their tongue in disgust.

Thapu nudged her forward, indicating they

should get away from the newcomer, but Olivia hesitated. Ms. PT-A's words came back to her, and her cheeks flushed with guilt at the idea of leaving the alien behind—especially since he was heading toward the wrong end of the exhibition. Before she could second-guess herself, she called ahead, "Hey, Karal?"

Karal's eight eyes dangled her way.

"Over here." She gestured shyly, indicating the correct virtual set where they needed to go.

Thapu nudged her, giving her a what-did-you-do-that-for look, before stepping through the bubble wall and leaving her to wait.

Olivia eyed the slimy rodent-like alien warily as he approached, then hurriedly stepped through the bubble wall after Thapu, still nervous about making friends with the newcomer.

"Why did y—," she scolded, then froze. What she saw next left her stunned. "Woooow!" she gasped, her jaw dropping.

Thapu grinned at her, and she sensed that Karal slid in behind them.

"Look at *that*!" she exclaimed, turning to check the expression on the other's faces, but Thapu and Karal broke down into pixels and vanished in a thick undergrowth of dark-green leaves and gnarled branches. Massive trees built up into a star-sprinkled night. Rich smells of flowers and earth filled the air. The forest came alive with the sound of hidden creatures: hooting, chirping, clicking, growling...

"You are on your own," the comforting museum-voice said through Olivia's earpiece. "Welcome to the deadly planet, Alluvium. Experts from the Exhibitus Museum selected the following scenes from the Professor Nando Pazorri Special Archive Collection of Video Feeds. You will walk in the hero's footsteps, experience his discovery of the Exostar and suffer his untimely death at the hands of the vicious Atun'ket Tribe. This state-of-the-art exhibit is brought to you by *Wanderer's Supermarkct*, your one-stop-shop for intergalactic deals. Enjoy!"

Click.

The museum-voice logged off.

ALLUVIUM
PLANET LOCATED IN
THE GOLDILOCKS ZONE
OF THE EXOSTAR SYSTEM
MILKY WAY GALAXY
INTEREST: HOME OF THE EXOSTAR

CHAPTER 3 *Cannibals*

Her heart beating wildly, Olivia listened to the unfamiliar sounds of the alien forest. She searched for Thapu and Karal with her eyes, but they had vanished into their own virtual bubbles. Although she had only been there for a couple of seconds, already, she felt disoriented.

Realizing she was truly alone, her breath quickened and came out loud in her ears. She could even hear an echo of it. *No, not an echo.* She tensed. Someone else was breathing as hard as she was! *There's someone else in here with me!*

Whirling around, she came face to face with a man heading straight towards her, an arm-length knife swinging in her direction.

Shrieking, Olivia stumbled and fell.

The man in beige safari clothes and a curious hat with a net hanging from the back of it, sliced off a luscious branch and stomped forward with his big boots, stepping straight through Olivia.

"Eek!" Olivia rolled over and got to her feet. *Virtual reality!* She reminded herself. *It's just a virtual reality scene.*

Already, the man had advanced through the thick shrub behind her, his back drenched in sweat. He stopped and turned around, and Olivia's heart skipped a beat. She recognized the deep-set eyes, the strong cheekbones, and the tanned complexion of her teenage heartthrob. She was standing before Professor Nando Pazorri himself! And he was staring straight at her.

"Come along, then!" he said gruffly, sounding impatient.

Olivia blinked, then realized that he was speaking to a group of men who were huffing and puffing up the mountain. She approached the Professor and, instantly, her MT device connected to his own so that, now, she was seeing things through his eyes. It was as if she was standing in the explorer's shoes!

"Cooool!" she breathed, thrilled by the prospect and suddenly feeling like a space explorer herself. She wondered if Thapu and Karal were experiencing the same thing.

The Professor studied the semblance of a path ahead of him that led through the tropical forest up to a flat area cut out in the flank of a mountain. The flickering fires of a native village were visible through the brush. He turned to face the sweaty little group that followed him. "Get along with it!" He spoke impatiently. "I'm doing all the hard work here. You think it's easy, slicing a way for you through the jungle with this thing?" He held up the long, sharp knife.

One of the men glanced up at him but, in doing so, lost his balance. A massive suitcase slid off his shoulders and hit the ground, shattering whatever it contained inside.

"Blistering ions, Brenol!" the Professor exploded. "There goes my mother's tea set."

The man called Brenol didn't seem to care much. He flopped onto the suitcase and wiped the sweat off his brow with the back of his arm. "Are we there yet?" he puffed.

The Professor's other four companions stopped, swaying under the weight of their loads, and glanced hopefully at the explorer.

"You fools! The natives are *right there*!" the Professor snapped, jabbing a finger up the hill. "Did you not see the speared heads down below? We could be dealing with cannibals! If we aren't careful, we could end up being their next meal!"

Brenol shrugged and pulled out a weapon, making Olivia flinch at its sight.

"So what? We'll give them a piece of our mind. I doubt they have laserbolts."

At the sight of the nasty weapon, the Professor took a couple of large strides and snatched it out of Brenol's hand. "What are you doing with this? I told you: no weapons! What were you think—" He broke off.

The thick underbrush rippled with sound and movement. Torches cast long shadows into the dark forest, closing in around them.

The Professor froze.

Native aliens materialized between the trees, holding sharp-looking spears that glinted in the torchlight.

No one moved.

With extreme care, the Professor aimed his camera at the aliens. When still no one twitched or spoke, he whispered—very gently, very slowly—into his camera. "First contact has been made with the locals." He paused. When nothing happened, he raised his voice a notch, listing his observations. "The locals are thin but not unhealthy. They have two arms and two legs; four-fingered hands. Three eyes, with the third one placed in the middle of their forehead. Their noses are tiny and their lower jaw sticks out over the top one, revealing pointy teeth. The males wear impressive headgear, skirts made of multicolored feathers, and necklaces made from leaves and silver flowers. Their skin is covered in a variety of beige, brown, and black fur, leaving only their faces, hands, and feet exposed, and—yuck!—that flesh is covered in some kind of smelly white paint."

Olivia blocked her nose, her stomach heaving at the stench.

The explorer lifted his hand to zoom in on the white paint.

This time, the movement sent the aliens into a frenzy. They lifted their spears, making particularly effective growling sounds.

Olivia cringed.

The Professor's companions huddled together, swaying under the weight of the suitcases they were carrying, yet too afraid to make a sudden movement by letting them go.

The Professor stood his ground. Finally, he took a deep breath and said, "Attempting contact."

Very slowly, very carefully, he fished out a finger-sized lighter from his breast pocket and clicked a button on its side. A small flame burst to life on top of it.

"Oooh!" The tribesmen jumped back, eyes wide.

"Oldest trick in the book," the Professor whispered smugly into his MT device. "Lighters always impress primitive societies."

Olivia raised an eyebrow. The lighter trick was so old-fashioned. Since then, the Interstellar Alliance had laid out strict rules on how to attempt first contact with alien civilizations. For fear of disrupting the culture or spreading previously unknown diseases, it could take decades of observation before a first move was even envisioned.

One of the tribesmen, who must have been their Chief, approached the Professor's little flame and watched it with his three eyes, then exchanged excited comments with his men. <Terra!> he repeated excitedly in his guttural language. <Terra! Terra!> It triggered a great change in them. They dropped at the Professor's feet and raised their arms toward him in apparent reverence.

<Terra,> they kept repeating.

"Terra," the Professor muttered. "We have established our first word with the inhabitants of the Exostar planet, and it is *God.*"

Shivering in excitement, Olivia barely had time to wonder how the explorer could have deduced the meaning of *Terra* when there was a sudden switch in the scenery. Now she found herself in a straw hut, facing the Professor's flustered but determined face. A shiver ran down her spine at his closeness. It was as if they were both sitting cross-legged, facing each other, and he was about to tell her an important secret. She leaned forward, even though she knew he had removed his MT device from around his ear and placed it in front of him.

"Professor Nando Pazorri, fifth expedition, log 327.6, day 2," he announced, nodding in satisfaction at the camera. "Hi, Mom. I'm recording this message through the tiny, high-tech earpiece you gave me. You know? The one you said was called a Mass Transfer device? That new, cutting-edge technology invented by the Civicus mega-corporation MADAT? The one you said I had to accept at the request of the Enillon government as a show of good faith towards the people of Civicus, our new interstellar allies?"

He looked away for a second as if thinking, then closed in abruptly on the camera so that Olivia saw one green eye staring back at her.

"Honestly? Feels more likely a spying device, if you ask me," he said. "What's up, Civicus? Are you snooping on me?" His eye stared at the camera; then he pulled back slowly with an accusing glare. He shrugged. "Whatever. I'll take all the help I can get, Mom. I mean, these expeditions are so expensive, so expensive." He trailed off, pressing his fingers against his eyes as if suddenly despairing. "Take the IQURUS, Mom. Do you have any idea how expensive it is to keep that thing flying? It's the only form of interstellar transport efficient enough to take me out of the Magnus Star Cluster without me having to experience a nasty time dilation.

"Imagine! Without the IQURUS, I could travel for three months, only to return and discover that two centuries have passed away back home. I know I told you before, Mom, but this is really important. Gravity on the surface of a planet makes time pass faster than it does in space. This is a well-known scientific fact. Quantum traveling is the only way for me to avoid this cumbersome problem. It's the only way for me to make discoveries and deliver them to you in a *timely* manner, you understand? So, could you, like, send me some more modicums before I run out? Could you, Mom? Please?"

Olivia pulled back, shocked. It was as if the young adult Professor had just asked her to lend him money. She furrowed her brow, not knowing what to think about this unexpected side of the great explorer.

The Professor paused, a grave expression on his face. "And discoveries, you will get, Mom. Pay attention, now. The planet I have just discovered has a long, promising future. It is green, teeming with forests, oceans, and alien life. You know how rare it is to find such a tree-covered rock in space!

"Also, the planet has a single bright blue sun, which I have named: Exostar. You know what that means, right? *Exo* because it means *external*; *external* because the star lies *outside* the Magnus Star Cluster and la-di-dah." He waved a hand dismissively. "I have not yet named the planet, though."

He dabbed the sweat from his forehead with the back of his hand, hesitating. "Look, Mom, I know we talked about calling any new planets I found, *Pazorri* or *Maria Gloriosa*, but I was thinking more along the lines of *Nando-2* or even *Nandini*—you know, Dad's nickname for me? What do you think? Or maybe, while I wait for you to get back to me, I'll ask the natives what they called it..." He bit his lower lip, frowning. "Yes, I think I'll do that. It will look respectful in my thesis. I can always change it later."

Olivia sighed, frustrated. What was this about a thesis? And why would the Professor impose a name on a planet that probably already had one? When would she get to the fun stuff?

She crossed her arms and forced herself to be patient. At least, her attention so far had offered her the answer to another homework question: she had found the meaning of *Exostar*.

CHAPTER 4 *Alluvium*

Thapu groaned and wished he had Olivia's patience. He could bet on it that she had already completed half the homework.

"But I found something better," he muttered vengefully. After pressing some virtual commands that his MT device had projected before his eyes, he had found a fast-forward button in the Professor Pazorri Special Archive Collection of Video Feeds. Now, he was pressing that button, forwarding, pausing, forwarding, pausing, zooming through the Professor's ramblings.

"Log 332.4, day 3. I learned the name of the tribe, Mom. They call themselves the Atun'ket."

Thapu watched some videos of the Professor's life among the fascinating tribe.

In one instance, the Professor asked the Chief about the severed heads on spears at the bottom of the mountain, to which the Chief shrugged and replied that the tribe living on the neighboring mountain kept raiding them. It had been important to teach them a lesson about courtesy and respect.

The Professor later said that he wondered why the neighbours would be raiding them. It wasn't like there was anything interesting to steal.

The Chief used a word that was unknown to the Professor. It sounded like *yummy* and, after some questioning, the Professor deduced that it meant *cannibal.* "It would seem that the Atun'ket ate their neighbors," he whispered hoarsely into his earpiece.

Then there were videos of the Professor trudging through the forest, which was thick and hot and full of creepy-crawlies. It teemed with dangerous plants and animals. The Professor said one wrong step, and he risked getting mauled, fatally stung, or buried alive in mud pits.

The Atun'ket didn't seem to mind, however. Whenever they prepared to enter the jungle to hunt for food, they would smile and say reverently in their native tongue, <Terra,> as if they were peacefully submitting their lives to the will of their God.

Next, Thapu paused on a humiliating incident when the Chief offered the Professor his daughter in marriage. Fortunately, she seemed as disgusted by his bare skin as he was with her furry hide, and, later—his face flushed—the Professor explained that she must have convinced her father to cancel the wedding because the Chief never mentioned it again.

Thapu snorted and shook his head, pressing the FORWARD button, until a scream made him jump out of his wits. He pressed PLAY...

The Professor woke up screaming in his hut. In an instant, the whole village rushed to his side, asking what was wrong, where did it hurt, did he have a nightmare, was he dying?

"My nose! Something stabbed my nose!" he wailed.

Whack!

A loud noise made the crowd whirl around. The Chief stood at the back of the hut with the Professor's boot in his hand. He pressed the boot against the wall, then held it up for all to see. Everyone burst out laughing. The Chief brought the boot close to the Professor's watery eyes, and Thapu noticed a tiny, bright-orange meskito crushed on its sole.

Hearty guffaws of laughter filled the village. One after the other, the tribespeople left the Professor's hut until only the grinning Chief remained. He crouched down beside the Professor and held up a mirror.

The explorer's red cheeks turned ashen. His nose had swollen to the size of a plum and began to droop down over his lips. Tears streamed down his cheeks.

The Chief released a pouch from his feather skirt, plunged his fingers into it, and spread some white, smelly goo onto the Professor's fingers. He pointed at the creamy substance, then at the cruel insect, then at the Professor's nose.

"Log 336.9, day 31. Mom, this is preposterous! Look at me! *Look* at me! I have to live with poo on my face! This stinky white muck is made from hippopus dung, Mother. *Hippopus dung!* Don't you *dare* make any of my logs public, Mom. Promise me you won't! The thought makes me sick to my stomach. I can't handle this another day. I want to go home; I've had enough! Why won't you accept my thesis? It's a thousand pages long! It's the longest homework I've ever written! How much longer does it have to be?"

Thapu roared with laughter.

"Log 338.1, day 34. Mom, there's nothing

else here. I know you want something unique, something mind-blowing, but there's nothing else here except for a festering, boiling jungle. I want a hot bath, Mom. I want Dad's mashed potato and veggie roast. I want to stroll around the university grounds and buy a cup of mollusk-infused tea at the local café. Please, Mom, can you just accept my thesis so I can come home?"

"Log 339.3, day 37. Mom, my team is useless. Why did you make me bring that Brenol-what's-his-name? He wants a pay raise, Mom. Now they all want a pay raise. They say I'm making them stay longer than expected. What am I supposed to tell them? Can you send over those modicums now?"

"Log 341.6, day 38. Mom, are you getting my messages? I know they take two days to reach you, but still... Does this thing even work? I mean, this MT-thingy is really handy when it comes to understanding the Atun'ket. It records any new word, works out its meaning, and translates whatever the tribespeople are saying directly into my ear. It's pretty efficient. But other than that, I don't even know if it's sending my messages. Did you talk to those benefactors? You're the Head of the Pazorri University, Mom. Can't you do something?"

"Log 343.1, day 42. Mom? Hello?"

With every passing log, the poor Professor looked more and more haggard. His hair sprouted out on top of his head like rays emanating from a star; his beard grew long and thick. He became thinner, and his naked torso became encrusted with hippopus dung.

Feeling slightly nauseated, Thapu forwarded the video. He wanted to get to the great discovery but also knew what that meant for the poor Professor. It didn't take long. On day 69, Thapu found the Professor gazing into the camera with a very troubled look on his face.

"Log... er...—he mumbled a random number—Mom... I... I discovered something. I... I don't understand. Mom, if you hear this, I need to know. You would know. You are the specialist in A'hmun history..." He leaned into the camera, a slightly crazed look in his eyes, and Thapu leaned forward, too.

"I learned the name of the planet," he admitted, glancing nervously about his little shack. "Listen to this! The Atun'ket call their planet: Alluvium. *Alluvium*, Mother!" He looked incredulous. "Isn't that an A'hmun word? In our language, Alluvium means 'a deposit of clay that produces fertile soil'. I mean, the name is fitting for this planet, but... It's an A'hmun word! How can that be? Is it a coincidence?

"Have I wasted months in this place when it turns out our distant relatives already traveled here before? Have they, Mom? Did our spacefaring ancestors discover this planet in the past?"

He swung back and forth, his brow deeply furrowed. "Am I not the first discoverer of Alluvium? Am I going to lose ownership of it? I need answers, Mom! I've checked our A'hmun logs, going back several generations. I've checked everything! There isn't a single mention of Alluvium in our history records from before our people settled permanently on Enillon. But what if I'm wrong? What am I going to tell my men, Mom? That I made them waste their time here for nothing?"

He slapped his hands against his cheeks, looking horrified. "And what about my thesis? What's going to become of my thesis? What if my homework gets torn to shreds by a peer historian who already knows about the existence of Alluvium? What if he calls me a fraud? Please, Mom, tell me you haven't heard of Alluvium before. Please, I need to know... Am I, or am I not, the first A'hmun explorer to set foot on

Alluvium?"

CHAPTER 5 *The Lost Space Treasure*

Thapu's heart raced, and he began to sweat. The very next log made goosebumps rise on his arms. He opened his eyes wide, taking in the details of the Professor's hut, smelling the old crusty hippopus dung, and listening to the hooting of exotic birds outside.

He faced the Professor, who was staring wide-eyed back at him through the camera, a forgotten feather swinging loosely on top of his thick hair. "Log... Ah, whatever! Mom! Something's happening! The Atun'ket Chief is going to adopt me into the tribe tonight! He's going to tell me the secret of Alluvium! It's something big! I can tell! The whole tribe is whispering about it when I approach them. Something's going to happen, Mom. I can feel it!"

Thapu bounced up and down in nervous anticipation. "C'mon! C'mon!" The virtual reality around the boy was replaced by a large fire burning in the middle of a clearing. The logs crackled, releasing sparkles that rose into the starry night. The Atun'ket Chief and the Professor sat, side by side, on a rocky slab covered in soft animal skins, their faces reflecting the dancing flames. The tribe sat in silence around the fire.

The Professor, along with Thapu, leaned in to listen.

The Chief munched on a pointy red fruit, his gaze lost on the fire. Then, he spoke in his native tongue, his voice deep and grave, and the translation dripped into Thapu's ear through his MT device. <Padremis the Creator, God of Atun'ket, come from the sky in great spirit-bird called the Terra Vault. Like your bird, but much bigger and much more beautiful.> He nodded wisely to himself, lost in thought, while the Professor scowled.

"Bigger and more beautiful, huh?" he mumbled, snatching the fruit the Chief was handing him. He tore into it with his teeth, grumbling, and instantly burst into tears. Gagging and coughing, the explorer stuck out his tongue, squinting at the innocent-looking fruit through wet eyes. "Fire-chili!" he rasped.

Thapu stuck out his own tongue, almost physically feeling the burning sensation as well.

The Chief took the fire-chili from him, still staring into the fire, completely ignorant of the Professor's struggle. He took another bite. <Padremis the Creator give planet name of Alluvium. Padremis the Creator bring with him greatest treasure in universe.> Tears streamed down his cheeks as he munched absentmindedly. <In his almighty grace, he share his treasure of Terra Vault with us to watch over for all eternity.>

The Chief straightened, punched his chest with a balled fist, and then hiccupped. <For six-thousand years, Atun'ket watch over gift, hoping Padremis the Creator return to see the good we have done with it, that we are grateful for celestial treasure and take good care of it.>

The Chief then lifted his glazed eyes towards the plate-sized moon shining over the mountains. He hiccupped again. <We thought you Creator God, but you not ask about great diamond. Very disappointing.>

The Professor gagged on the water he was downing. "WHA'...?" he squeaked, his tongue sticking out of his mouth. "Wha' diamond?"

The Chief ignored him and began to chant his way through a song to the beat of his hiccups. The tribe hummed along.

> <Fields of diamonds, columns of gold, (hic)
> Ceilings of emeralds, a wonder to behold.
> Fountains of silver, rubies they hold. (hic)
> Share your treasure,
> oh, Keeper of the Terra Vault.
> (hic)>

The Chief fell silent, his face glowing with religious fervor.

The Professor stared at the old man, eyes bulging. Almost as an afterthought, he pulled his burning tongue back into his mouth. "A god? Who came in a mathive spacethip? Filled with gold and rubieth and emeraldth? Six thousand years ago? He gave you a diamond? Wha'ever for? Wha' diamond? Where ith it? Why haven't I theen it yet? Where thiz 'iamond? Where thiz treathure?"

The Chief's three eyelids drooped. <Great treasure,> he mumbled, his body slumping against the Professor's side, <is lost in space.> The Chief's head fell onto the explorer's lap.

"WHAT TREASURE?" the Professor and

Thapu yelled in unison, but all they got was a loud snore.

CHAPTER 6 *Diamond*

Professor Nando Pazorri paced up and down his hut. He stopped by the window, looked out, then paced again. He spoke into his MT device, holding it in his hands and pointing his camera at his face. He looked a lot better than in the previous log and had even trimmed his beard. "Six thousand years ago, a mysterious spaceship called the Terra Vault landed on Alluvium. The spaceship was so stacked with treasures that its captain—some guy named Padremis—casually gifted the Atun'ket with a diamond." He trailed off.

"A diamond! For the Atun'ket! Why give a diamond to a tribe in a jungle? It's not like they can do anything with it. They have nothing to buy! They have no stores, no money, no high-tech weapons, and nothing to barter with. All they care about is this animal-infested forest of theirs. And yet, this diamond was given to them the way I have given them plastic spoons and a cheap flashlight." He stopped pacing.

"This Padremis must have been wealthy, indeed, to have given away such a precious stone like that!"

<OOM, OOM, OOM...> Indigenous chanting traveled up the path.

The Professor rushed to the window again, speaking hurriedly into the camera. "This is it, Mom! The Chief is going to show me the diamond today! This is the breakthrough we've been waiting for! I will be going down in the book of Renowned Interstellar Explorers, Mom. You'll be proud!"

The camera swung up as he attached the device to his ear. "What should I give them in exchange for the diamond, Mom? They have no use for it. Too bad your tea set is broken. Maybe I can give them a water pump instead. Or fever medicine, or a good cutlery set..." He paused. "Yes, the cutlery set! I'll tell Brenol to bring it over later."

Olivia flushed. A cutlery set? In exchange for a diamond? Somehow, that didn't seem fair.

The Professor turned, flinging open his bamboo door.

<OOM, OOM, OOM...> A procession of tribespeople chanted the eerie tune as they followed their Chief. For once, the old man looked solemn. He wasn't wearing his usual boyish grin with his pointy popcorn teeth jutting out of his lower jaw.

The dozen or so strong natives that followed him wore long black feathered skirts and headsets made from skulls. The latter were equally decorated with black feathers that flowed down their backs.

The Professor shut the door suddenly, slumping back against it. "What if the skulls didn't belong to victims of the neighbors but to members of the tribe? What if they were," —he swallowed visibly— "*sacrificed*? Mom, I'm scared. The whole thing's creepy..." Olivia could hear him breathing hard. "Great quarks! Mom! The Chief said he was disappointed that I'm not Padremis the Creator. What if they want to sacrifice *me*? What if this is a sacrificial ceremony instead of a tribal baptism?"

Goosebumps rose on Olivia's arms. *Poor Professor!* She already knew how the story would end.

The camera swung down, and the Professor uncovered the laserbolt hidden away in the folds of his feathered skirt. The chanting natives approached the hut.

"I'll keep this close, just in case..." The Professor tapped the weapon, then covered it up again. He blew air out of his cheeks. "It's okay. I'll be okay, Mom. I must get that diamond. You'll see. I'll be home soon. And I'll be *rich*!" He swung around and opened the door again.

The Chief waited solemnly for the Professor to step out of his hut, then placed a skull on top of the explorer's head.

The Professor followed the procession, walking behind the Chief while flanked by the chanting natives. They headed up a mountain path, treading slowly through a thickening forest. Tree trunks became thicker and taller, shutting out light and sound. The group fell silent until they reached a gateway made of gray rocks stacked on top of each other, beyond which stretched a gloomy tunnel that led deep into the mountain. A larger rock, placed to the side of the entrance, had an ancient inscription chipped into it:

▸[][]⍰▾[]☑♠□□

[]▶[][]❓▼[]☑♠□

❓▼[]☑□□♠▶□□

▶[]☑♠□□□□♠

[]▶[]☑□♠

At its sight, the natives burst into song—the same one as before—allowing the explorer to rest his camera on the symbols for a long moment.

Passing through the gateway, they entered a dim corridor that led to a cave. The roof of the cave was open to the sky, but the roots of massive trees bordering the circular ledge almost shut off any natural light. Water dripped down the rocky walls, and ferns cascaded down from above. The atmosphere was thick and oppressive.

The tribespeople took their places in a circle around the Professor, making blunt, repetitive movements with their spears. <OOM, OOM, OOM...> they chanted. The sharp spears glinted in the gloom, and Olivia tensed, sensing the end was near.

The Professor took a step back, finding himself blocked by a knee-high rock jutting out into the middle of the cave. He could see his cracked reflection in it.

Silence fell over the group. Everyone waited. Olivia held her breath. Then, a ray of light from the planet's Exostar slipped into the cave from above, falling on the rock next to the explorer. It lit up.

Olivia let out a shriek.

As more sunlight filtered through, the rock turned into the most beautiful thing she had ever seen in her life.

The rock wasn't a rock. It was a diamond, the biggest, most beautiful diamond she had ever laid eyes on. It caught the rays and broke them into a thousand prisms that reflected across the cave. Its heart shone with a clear, blue glow as bright as the planet's sun.

"Great quarks!" the explorer gasped. "It... It's beautiful! It... it's... I... I can't believe it! It's like a chunk of the blue sun had been chopped off and dropped here into this dark hole. No... not *like* the sun. This *is* the sun! This *is* the Exostar! *My* Exostar!" The Professor broke into a babbling mess. He couldn't stop. "I'm going to be rich beyond belief, Mom! I will be the wealthiest man in the whole Magnus Star Cluster. No. Forget that. I'm going to be the wealthiest man in the entire galaxy! Mother... You will drop to your knees in admiration. You will revere me. *All* will revere me!"

<OOM, OOM, OOM...> The natives' chant

began again and grew louder; their dance around the diamond—and the Professor—became more frenzied.

Olivia's back became drenched in sweat.

"Gotta find the rest. Gotta find the rest of the lost space treasure. Must find the Terra Vault..." The Professor glanced down and curled a trembling hand around his laserbolt. Then, he looked up and locked eyes with the Chief. "I'll give you anything—*anything*—in exchange for the diamond. What do you want? Do you want a palace? A quantum rocket? Ten quantum rockets? I'll give them to you. Name your price!"

<OOM, OOM, OOM...> the Chief chanted, never breaking the vibrant rhythm of his thumping feet. <The Professor have hippopus dung in his head,> he said, still dancing around. He broke into a grin that revealed his pointy teeth. <Great diamond of Padremis the Creator is holy. Padremis the Creator give diamond to the Atun'ket. Diamond is life and heart of Atun'ket. No diamond, no Atun'ket, no Alluvium. Treasure of Terra Vault is not for trade.> He lifted his spear the Professor's way, his feverish eyes bearing down on the explorer.

The sun's rays slid away from the hole, locking them into a sweltering gloom.

The Professor reached for his MT device and switched off the video feed.

EXHIBITUS
POLITICAL AND CULTURAL CENTER
OF THE INTERSTELLAR ALLIANCE
MAGNUS STAR CLUSTER
MILKY WAY GALAXY
INTEREST: ARTIFICIAL MOON ORBITING THE
WANDERING PLANET GALLIVANTO.

CHAPTER 7 *Lunch*

Olivia screamed. One second, the vicious Atun'ket Chief was aiming his spear at her, showing his nasty teeth, and the next, the virtual cave crashed around her in a cascade of pixels, leaving her in total darkness.

She could hear somebody breathing hard into her MT device. Then, there were thudding footsteps, and the darkness split open into a pixelated jungle that built up before her. She watched, terrified, through the Professor's video feed, as he crashed through the bushes and tripped over tree roots. Spurred on by his panic, Olivia began to run, too, forgetting that she was in a virtual set at the Exhibitus Museum.

Fierce howls and growls followed close by. Olivia turned in unison with the Professor's camera to see the cannibals at her heels, waving sharp spears above their heads.

The explorer shrieked.

Olivia shrieked.

They burst through the thicket.

The Professor's quantum rocket appeared, parked in a clearing in the middle of the jungle.

"HEEELP!" he screamed, running for his life. "Open the airlock! QUICKLYYY!"

The door to the IQURUS slid open, and Brenol appeared with a blank look on his face.

The Professor was almost there. Spears thudded into the ground beside him.

Olivia's heart raced as she ran in his footsteps. Her teacher had mentioned something about proceeding to the EXIT sign blinking on her MT map. "The Exit! Where's the Exit?" she cried, frantically pressing her MT device to search for a way out of the Exhibition.

Brenol's eyes bulged when he spotted the

fierce Atun'ket emerging from the forest and heading toward the spaceship. He took a step back.

"No! Wait!" the Professor yelled. He stretched out his arms which carried something shaped like a hippopus baby. A ray of sun fell on the object, and it burst into a gazillion pinpricks of light. "EXOSTAR!" he shouted. "DIAMOOOND!"

Brenol froze, his eyes bulging.

Just then, there was a dull thud.

The Professor gargled. The diamond rolled out of the great explorer's arms just before he swayed and fell flat on his face. His MT device slipped off his ear, and miraculously, it continued filming at an awkward angle.

Brenol leaped off the spaceship, sprinted to the diamond which had rolled his way, and picked it up. He glanced at the fallen explorer, but when spears landed inches before his feet, he yelped and raced back into the spaceship.

Shortly after, the IQURUS took flight, sharp spears clanging harmlessly against its side. It lifted into the air and disappeared from the field of vision of the Professor's camera, leaving the great explorer behind.

Olivia was still running. An EXIT sign blinked in the right-hand corner of her MT device. Frantically, she flung herself to the right and slammed face-first into a wall. She dropped on her backside, stunned.

Around her, the virtual set disintegrated into a shower of pixels, and she found herself looking up at Ms. PT-A, whose face-screen broke into a tranquil smile. "Hello, Olivia. Did you have fun at the Exhib—"

Someone smashed into Olivia.

She barely had time to realize it was Thapu, before another kid tripped over them, covering them with his wet, gooey belly.

"YUUUCK!" Thapu burst out.

"Let me outta here!" Olivia yelled as the pile of arms, legs, and sliminess increased above her.

It took a while for a dozen dazed students to unknot themselves from each other and gather their senses. They picked themselves up and stared at each other. They were safe. They had not died on Alluvium. Cannibals had not eaten them. They had followed the great explorer in his footsteps, learned the ways of the Atun'ket, and discovered the Exostar. All in all, it had turned into the most exhilarating, mind-blowing adventure of their lives.

It took another hour before Museum Security was able to fish out the remaining lost students from the various virtual sets.

Once they were all accounted for, Ms. PT-A's body did a hundred-and-eighty-degree turn and hovered away from the Professor Nando Pazorri Exhibition. "Now, class," she said, "let's have lunch."

CHAPTER 8 *Interstellar Alliance*

Ms. PT-A closed the eight drawers of her lower body but had to twist her metallic hand into a hammer for the last one because Karal's lunchbox wouldn't fit. She slammed at the drawer several times until it clicked shut, tearing a piece of the lunchbox lid in the process.

A student giggled and tugged at the broken piece that hung limply to the side, while Ms. PT-A gathered the rest of the class in front of her.

"It's time," the robot teacher announced.

The students held their breath.

"Within this exhibit lies the Exostar," she said, pointing at a large spherical structure in the middle of the museum hangar. "From now on, I require you to be on your best behavior. The Exostar is the most guarded object in the entire Interstellar Alliance. We will line up calmly behind the waiting visitors.

"You will be scanned and identified before you can enter. You will see armed soldiers and security drones within the exhibit."

Thapu hopped from one leg to the other, eyeing the growing line of visitors to the exhibit.

Olivia cast him an annoyed look.

"The Exostar lies at the heart of the Exhibitus Museum," Ms. PT-A continued, "and the Exhibitus Museum, along with the government facilities of the Interstellar Alliance, lie inside the center of the artificial moon with the same name—Exhibitus. The hollow, round moon has multiple entry points for the seven planets of the Interstellar Alliance, adapted to each population and spaceship, with extremely tight controls, laserbolt cannons, and in-depth surveillance of MT devices. Needless to say, we are in the safest location of the entire Interstellar Alliance, so be warned that one false step could land you in jail for a very long time (I say '*you*' because my memory storage would simply be erased)."

The students glanced at each other.

Ms. PT-A joined the line of visitors on a conveyor belt with two rows of hovering chairs. The students followed obediently, stepping onto the moving carpet, then taking a seat one behind the other. "Now, who can tell me the meaning of the symbols above the entrance to the exhibit?" Ms. PT-A asked, facing them.

The children craned their necks and recognized the phosphorescent symbols above the main door.

▶[][]▨▾[]☑♠□□
[]▶[][]▨▾[]☑♠□
▨▾[]☑□□♠▶□□
▶[]☑♠□□□□♠
[]▶[]☑□♠

They chanted automatically:

Fields of diamonds, columns of gold,
ceilings of emeralds, a wonder to behold.
Fountains of silver, rubies they hold.
Share your treasure,
oh, Keeper of the Terra Vault.

Visitors smiled at them knowingly. Everyone knew the song about the legendary Lost Space

Treasure from their childhood.

Since the conveyor belt advanced slowly—the rubber floor squeaking under the effort of carrying so many visitors over the years—Ms. PT-A dove straight into a history lesson, making some students scowl at her.

"If you remember our lesson from last week, then you will understand this exhibit's importance. You see, it is the Exostar that almost tore apart the civilizations of the Magnus Star Cluster. Yet, the Exostar also led to the birth of the Interstellar Alliance, which lies within this Cluster.

"When Brenol Trock—mechanic on the Professor's IQURUS—brought back the Exostar, he was hailed as a hero. But word soon spread of the mighty diamond, and jealousy and greed festered from one end of the Cluster to the other. Every civilized planet of the Cluster tried to lay claim to the diamond in the hopes of becoming rich and powerful. Enillon maintained that the Exostar belonged to them because their citizen had found it. Civicus said that the Professor could not have traveled to Alluvium without the IQURUS they had lent him. Vunkotune said the IQURUS would not have existed without the metal extracted from their planet. Plethora said that without Brenol Trock—a citizen of theirs—

the diamond would never have made it back to the Cluster, and so on.

"As you all know, this led to the Exostar War, which lasted one hundred and fifty years. When the warring planets had finished trying to steal the Exostar from each other, and realized that no one was coming out as the winner, they decided to sign a peace deal.

"On the year zero a.i.a.[1] of the Fourth Quadrant, the seven major planets of the Magnus Star Cluster signed the Exostar Peace Act, thereby creating the Interstellar Alliance. It was decided that the Exostar would belong to all, never again to be sold, possessed, or stolen by anyone. Rather, it would remain untouched, only to be admired and enjoyed by every species in the Cluster.

"And so, the artificial moon Exhibitus was created as a beacon of governance, knowledge, friendship, and peace, with the Exhibitus Museum in its center. And at its heart, the Exostar was placed." She turned to face the spherical exhibit. "As long as the Exostar remains here, there will be peace," she finished.

The class straightened in their seats. This particular history lesson had been boring last week, but today, it became more exciting and *real*,

---

[1] a.i.a.: After Interstellar Alliance

so they hung on to her every word.

Since they still hadn't arrived at the entrance, Ms. PT-A went on to cover some general facts. "Who can tell me the names of the seven civilized planets of the Interstellar Alliance—eight, if you include Exhibitus?"

"Me, me!" a boy at the back stabbed his finger in the air.

Ms. PT-A nodded once. "Yes, Saami?"

He counted with his fingers. "Exhibitus, Gallivanto, Enillon, Plethora, Civicus-1, -2 and -3, Gemelo, Vunkotune and... and... Stuupidus."

His companions burst out laughing. Stuupidus was a common nickname among youngsters for the sixth planet of the Interstellar Alliance.

"SAAMI!" Ms. PT-A scolded. The students cringed at the sudden raised volume coming from their MT devices.

Saami went crimson and thrust a hand to his mouth. His eyes rolled to the side until they fell on Karal.

"Apologize to Karal at once!" Ms. PT-A said in the same, high volume.

"S-sorry, K-Karal," Saami mumbled, sliding further down in his seat.

Ms. PT-A turned to the alien child. "Karal,

will you kindly teach your companions the correct name of your planet?"

The students turned to face Karal, sitting alone at the back. A blubbering alien speech came out of his mouth, contrasting oddly with the clear, confident, and friendly common Alliance translation that they heard through their earpiecc.

<My planet is called Lluunides—not Stuupidus,> Karal corrected wisely. <Lluunides is a large moon that orbits a gas planet, and this gas planet, in turn, orbits a pulsar. A pulsar is a tiny, compact star that is a remnant of a supernova. My star exploded billions of years ago, and the planets and moons that orbit it now were formed by leftover material clumping together.

<Lluunides is the garbage collector of the Interstellar Alliance. Without Lluunides, the rest of your planets would be drowning in their own litter.> Karal's mouth stretched into a wide grin, then he proceeded to chomp on a broken piece of the lid from his lunchbox.

The children turned to face their teacher again, looking slightly sick.

"Excellent, Karal," Ms. PT-A complimented him. "You get twenty minutes in the IQURUS cockpit," She flicked a finger Karal's way, and Karal's MT device pinged as he received the bonus minutes while some students grumbled, "Not fair!"

"And you get to travel at the back, in the windowless fourth class," Ms. PT-A began, addressing a pale-faced Saami, but before she could transmit the order, an Exhibitus Security robot barked beside her, "Identifications, please!"

They were about to enter the exhibit.

CHAPTER 9 *Exostar*

It was said that no one who laid eyes on the Exostar came out the same again. Oliva soon discovered that this statement was true.

When the conveyor belt transported her into the sphere containing the Exostar, her mind went blank. Her eyes could not comprehend what they were seeing. The diamond, which was about half her size, hovered in the center of the sphere, bathing her soul in its blue magnificence. The conveyor belt circled it, coming in through one door and exiting it through another placed right next to the first one.

The slow-moving carpet advanced with not a soul budging or speaking. The atmosphere was a reverent one, full of wonder and awe. Was it real?

Were they dreaming? How was it possible that such a gorgeous object could exist?

Ms. PT-A's voice droned on.

Olivia wished she would stop talking. She was spellbound by the diamond, and all she wanted was to gape at it reverently.

"The exhibit is split into three floors," Ms. PT-A explained. "The top floor is for visitors coming from planets with low gravities such as Gemelo and Civicus; the middle floor is for those with high gravities such as Enillon, Lluunides, Vunkotune, and Plethora; and the lower floor is— of course—for the water people of Gallivanto. Students, be warned that it is forbidden to go prancing about on the top floor or swimming in the lower floor. You will remain on our appointed middle floor at all times!

"Organizing the inside of the exhibit turned out to be quite a complex matter," she continued. "The people of Civicus, who are known to complain about everything, were not happy at the prospect of having to see the Exostar from above until they realized they would be sharing their tunnel with the ancient, wise, and noble aliens from Gemelo.

"The beings from Gemelo, on the other hand, protested at the idea that they had to use visibility shields. But Exhibitus Security would not hear of having it any other way. As you all know, Gemelans live in a light spectrum that is not visible to the other alien species. Exhibitus Security could not very well have invisible, ghostly forms wandering about the facilities. The visibility shields revealed the presence of Gemelans' bodies to others, which solved that problem.

"And the tunnel below us is designed for the people of Gallivanto," Ms. PT-A explained.

Olivia gazed briefly at the brightly-colored fish and siren folk swimming below her feet, pressing their slimy scales against the glass.

"The tunnel is the biggest one because it contains the most visitors. This is, of course, because Exhibitus orbits Gallivanto as its artificial moon. Gallivanteans are just a space-hop away from the Museum, which doesn't require expensive quantum travel on their part."

Under normal circumstances, Olivia would have been fascinated by this intriguing display of alien species. But not so, now. She had eyes only for the Exostar.

"Karal," Ms. PT-A warned the alien child. "Pick your jaw up off the floor, please."

Karal closed his gigantic mouth, but it soon

dropped open again.

There was not a single living being inside the exhibit who did not experience the same sequence of emotions.

First, Olivia experienced utter stupefaction, then one of aching need ('I must have the Exostar! The Exostar is mine! No one else can have it!'). Thirdly, a feeling of guilt ('But greed for the Exostar led to massive destruction, jealousy, death.'). And that thought was immediately followed once again with one of wonder and want.

The diamond was well named, she thought. *Exostar*, or *star from beyond*. It was easy to picture why the Professor had thought it was a piece of Alluvium's sun. Having seen the bright blue star first-hand in the virtual exhibition, Olivia felt in sync with the name.

Her thoughts wandered to the Lost Space Treasure.

The Lost Space Treasure was supposed to be a myth, a child's bedtime story. But the Exostar stood right before her, taunting that belief, making her imagination run wild.

As if reading her mind, Thapu approached her and whispered, "If the Exostar exists, then the Lost Space Treasure has to exist, too, hasn't it? The Exostar had to come from somewhere, right? So where's the rest of the treasure? Do you think the other gems mentioned in the song could be this big? This valuable?"

All Olivia could do was shake her head. She didn't know. But she wished she did.

Her eyes darted down and unintentionally fell on a museum panel that provided visitor information.

"Oh, quarks!" she muttered, realizing it contained an answer to one of the homework questions. She wanted to kick herself. Having been entranced by the Exostar, she had already missed half of the panels.

"Look at this." She read out a tiny footnote on the panel to Thapu. "Scholars from the Pazorri University discovered that the correct translation of the Atun'ket word *yummy* was *thief,* not *cannibal.* But seeing as treasure hunters had wiped out the Atun'ket Tribe by then, these same scholars ultimately concluded that it would be too cumbersome to try and correct the deeply ingrained popular belief that the Atun'ket were vicious cannibals."

"Wow!" Thapu gave a low whistle. "So, does that mean that the Atun'ket weren't cannibals, after all?"

Olivia frowned, deeply disturbed by the idea

that most of what she knew of the past might be a lie. "I don't know."

"It says that treasure hunters wiped out the tribe, so I guess we'll never know for sure," Thapu stated morosely.

"That's so sad! Why haven't they corrected the history records?" Olivia's heart squeezed. A clear image of the old Chief flashed in her mind, and she suddenly felt like she had lost a special friend or an important character in a good book to which she had unknowingly grown attached.

She realized that the old Chief and Karal had something in common: they had both frightened her at first, but once she had gotten to know them better, she had found that they had a lot to offer in terms of cultural knowledge and—perhaps—friendship.

"So, I guess they didn't eat the Professor, either," Thapu pouted.

"Thapu!" Olivia scolded him. "How can you be thinking of the Professor when a whole tribe was massacred? The Professor stole the Exostar from the Atun'ket, remember? They had every right to go after him."

"Pff. So what? They had no need for it. If the Professor hadn't taken it from them, we wouldn't be looking at it right now. You can't keep a diamond like that stashed away. It has to be shared and admired by all."

"Thapu!" Olivia glared at him. "You're so insensitive!" she began, but her eyes fell on the Exostar again, and she immediately felt a tug of longing. "It doesn't seem fair," she mumbled, fighting a guilty sense of need.

Ms. PT-A's voice trickled toward them from further down the tunnel. "Unfortunately, aside from the Professor's video feeds which were donated to the Pazorri Library by the explorer's mother, no other information exists about the legendary Lost Space Treasure," she was saying. "By the time the Exostar War ended and scientific expeditions were sent to Alluvium to find out more about the Treasure, the planet's oceans and forests had long since been raked barren by ruthless treasure hunters. Not a single Atun'ket remained—nor any living animal or plant, for that matter. The planet was dead, its surface destroyed by deep holes and gashes made by explosives.

"To make matters worse, an analysis from a single atom taken from the Exostar determined that the gem did not come from this galaxy. This is a dreadful conclusion! What if the Terra Vault returned to its former home—in another galaxy? Where could that be? How could anyone ever find it?"

Flustered tears filled Olivia's eyes. The Atun'ket were truly gone. The Space Treasure was indefinitely lost. *Such a waste!*

As they reached the end of the spherical exhibit, her chest burned with an inner fire. *If the Lost Space Treasure can never be found,* she thought, *and if the Exostar is all that remains of it, then it has to be protected at all costs.* Every single being who lays eyes on the diamond needs to know from now on and forever more that the Exostar is safe and that they can visit it at the Exhibitus Museum over and over again to their hearts' content.

Ms. PT-A's words echoed in Olivia's mind. *As long as the Exostar remains on Exhibitus, it guarantees peace.*

That was until the unthinkable happened: the diamond was stolen.

CHAPTER 10 *The Attack*

Thapu was angling his way to the back of the class so he could admire the Exostar a little longer when a catastrophic explosion tore into Exhibitus.

A massive earthquake rattled the artificial moon, flinging everybody to the ground. Earsplitting sounds of grinding metal drowned out the terrified screams. The room shook so hard it seemed like a giant God-child had decided to play ball with Exhibitus.

Vunkotunians, Gallivanteans, and A'hmuns landed in a messy heap on their respective floors. Emergency exits slammed shut while warning lights flashed and sirens wailed.

Ms. PT-A's pixel eyes turned to two X's, and her mouth turned to a large O as her computer-mind tried to figure out which emergency protocol she should apply in this type of situation.

After horrifying minutes, the shaking stopped. The dull crunching and grinding died down. Thapu held his breath.

Children wailed, their hands pressed to their ears. Adults straightened up, only to realize they were locked inside the exhibit. Their panicked shouts rose above each other. Robot guards that had been tossed in all directions, returned to their positions around the Exostar, weapons raised. Confused drones bobbed up and down, trying to recover a stable flight while scanning the visitors with angry red lights as they searched for the culprits.

Clunk!

Thapu glanced up.

Something hard had hit the outer core of the exhibit. Then, a sharp, white light pierced the metal hull from above. The laser beam fell on the children's tunnel, then on the floor that separated them from the lower level. Thapu scrambled to the side to avoid the knife-sharp ray, which began to cut a square opening in the roof of the exhibit. Only, it cut a similar-shaped hole in the children's tunnel and the floor that separated them from the water people.

The hole in the roof caused a pressure imbalance, sucking out every loose object surrounding the Exostar. Robot guards and drones—their metal arms and rotors tossing about—vanished through the hole without a sound.

Terror grasped the beings caught within the tunnels as the vacuum tried to suck them up. Water burst from the lower tunnel up to the middle one, splashing over Thapu's feet. He yelled and frantically grabbed onto the conveyor belt, feeling the strong tug of the vacuum. He would be flung into the void! He would drown in Gallivanto's water! He was doomed! This was the end!

Except, it wasn't.

The most unlikely hero came to the rescue.

Karal, who hung on to the tunnel wall by sticking his gooey butt to the window, used the suckers at the end of his tail to slide over to the hole. He flipped around and landed stomach-first into the opening.

Blop!

The hole was plugged.

The air no longer escaped from the tunnel, students let go of the conveyor belt, and water stopped rising from the lower to the middle level.

Visitors picked themselves up and stared at the alien child from Lluunides, who had just saved their lives.

Thapu stood carefully, astonished, then noticed Karal's struggle to avoid getting sucked out of the hole. His long tail tensed as it stretched the width of the tunnel, and the suckers at the end of it were already beginning to loosen from the glass.

"Olivia!" Thapu called, catching her looking his way. "Quickly!" He rushed to Karal's side and grabbed onto the alien.

Olivia did the same.

"Hang on, Karal!" Thapu yelled, grimacing under the effort.

Others arrived and held on to Karal's tail. But, even so, the air that escaped and spilled out into space extracted an enormous pull within the exhibit.

"Karal!" Thapu screamed, feeling him slip away from him.

Karal's eight eyes dangled his way in terror.

Just then, a plate-sized robot with its own set of suckers at the end of its spider-like legs made its way down from outside the tunnel. No sooner had it reached Karal than it spewed a transparent net over the hole. At once, the air stabilized, and everyone fell back, landing in a thin layer of water.

"Karal!" Olivia yelled, throwing her arms around the alien child. "Oh, thank you!"

Thapu patted him on the back giddily. "Thanks, buddy," he gasped, his legs feeling like jelly.

But they weren't out of trouble yet.

The laser beam switched off, there was a brief silence, and then armor-clad beings made their appearance.

The attackers dropped down through the hole in the ceiling, pointing arm-length canon-like weapons at the visitors. Their heavy boots were strapped to small drones that allowed them to fly from one end of the room to the other. They hovered around the Exostar, making sure no one moved.

More shielded bandits glided down into the exhibit. Although they had two arms and two legs, their gray battle suits and helmets made it impossible to tell who or what they were: humanoid, cyborg, android, animal, or something else.

There was no time to ponder further because now an ugly-looking metal clamp attached at the end of a chain descended into the room, stopping right above the Exostar.

Thapu let out a barely audible moan as he guessed the evil intent of the intruders. He could hear heavy fighting around the spherical room. "There must be more intruders outside the exhibit," he shouted, "and Exhibitus Security is fighting against them! They'll do everything possible to save the Exostar, won't they?" But the words died in his throat.

A last figure appeared—this one taller than the others and wearing a suit of white armor. The sight of the being made Thapu's blood run cold. The thing inside the armor dropped from the roof to the floor of the exhibit, wearing a small drone on each foot. Dark orange cloth went from the figure's wrists to its ankles, forming eerie wings folded under the arms, and the wearer's helmet had markings in the same orange tone presenting a skeletal face with an evil grin. The black compound eyes didn't help the fearsome look, and Thapu backed up at its sight.

Only Ms. PT-A seemed unfazed by this frightening presence. Had she found a protocol to deal with this type of threat? Then the teacher's XOX face turned to static, and an A'hmun face appeared on her screen. The man wore a military cap, a beige collar that reached just under his mouth, and black goggles. He turned briefly to speak to someone behind him. "Am I logged in? Can they hear me?" he asked.

Someone must have answered in the affirmative because the man turned to face the crowd in the exhibit again. "This is Commander Jacobus Noze, head of Exhibitus Security. You are in violation of code 1.a of the Exostar Peace Act. Surrender yourself!"

As if in defiance, the metal clamp lowered, releasing three sharp fingers over the Exostar. The fingers tightened around the diamond, then the powerful chain became taut, and the Exostar began to lift into the air.

"You are stealing the Exostar!" Commander Noze shrieked, stating the obvious. "That is an act punishable by atomization! Return the Exostar at once! You are surrounded!"

The diamond was lifted towards the ceiling, followed by half of the bandits. The remaining ones took place behind the figure, whose helmet grinned evilly at the Commander.

"Identify yourself!" the Commander blared, making everyone wince and reach for their MT devices to lower the volume.

The white-clad being rose to the level of Thapu and Olivia, facing them with its huge fly-like eyes. Then, it stretched its right arm and pointed straight at them as if condemning them.

The children cringed.

A raucous, scratching voice came out of its helmet, speaking the common Alliance tongue with a heavy accent. "We come from the darkest corner of your history," it said in a tone that was neither male nor female. "We come to haunt those who erased us from their memories. Will these younglings remember? Will you teach them?"

The being backed away just as the Exostar disappeared through the hole.

"The diamond belongs to us! The Terra Vault belongs to us!" the being shouted, rising after the gem. "Do not attempt to follow us, or you will suffer our vengeance!"

LUNA DUO
MOON ORBITING THE
WANDERING PLANET, GALLIVANTO
MAGNUS STAR CLUSTER
MILKY WAY GALAXY
INTEREST: TEMPORARY SEAT OF THE
INTERSTELLAR ALLIANCE

CHAPTER 11 *Peace in the Balance*

Five days later, Thapu walked down a hallway under a makeshift dome on Luna Duo, one of Gallivanto's many moons. Karal slid beside him, his gooey body leaving a wet trail on the posh carpet, while Olivia flanked the alien's other side, nervously glancing at them every ten seconds. They followed Ms. PT-A, who, in turn, was being guided by an Interstellar Alliance service droid.

Passing by a curved window, Thapu caught sight of the broken carcass of Exhibitus, floating a few space units away, and his blood went cold.

The massive Vunkotune warship that had struck the artificial moon five days ago lay deeply embedded into it, resembling a knife protruding from a heart.

Thapu looked away quickly, feeling weak in the knees. *I could have died there...*

He had barely slept since the attack. None of them had. They had been kept in confinement on an Alliance Hospital Ship—for their own safety, they were told—without being able to talk to or see their distressed parents, or anyone else, for that matter.

Then, on this day, the small group was suddenly transported from the hospital to Gallivanto's moon.

The service droid stopped abruptly, turning to face the double doors to its left. It checked that the others had caught up before swinging the doors open. A cacophony of voices engulfed the small group, making them freeze in the doorway.

The moon settlement, which had hastily been built after the attack, consisted of a transparent dome facing Gallivanto, the planet it orbited. The conference room lay in the center of the dome and was now crowded with beings from all over the Interstellar Alliance. There were tall, mysterious beings from Gemelo, blue-skinned aliens from Plethora, beige and brown-skinned A'hmuns from Enillon, robots from Vunkotune, and gooey blobs from Lluunides. The exotic sea creatures from Gallivanto wore transparent space suits filled with water to guarantee their survival. The crowd talked loudly, waving arms, eye stalks, and fins.

Olivia moaned fearfully. "They never said the whole Interstellar Alliance would question us!"

Thapu swallowed. No, indeed, no one had warned them.

Taking a hesitant step into the room, he shielded his eyes with his hand, letting them adjust to the glare coming from the blue sea planet, Gallivanto, which filled the view outside the glass dome. It crossed his mind that the attendees looked like upside-down flies stuck to a wall, illuminated by a massive light bulb.

A few people pointed their way, obviously recognizing them as the ones who had survived the attack. Thapu automatically huddled closer to his friends as he followed the service droid into the room.

To Thapu's dismay, Ms. PT-A figured this was a good time for an astronomy class. "Isn't this a wonderful view, students?" She said matter-of-factly, pointing upwards. "Gallivanto is known as the *Wandering Planet*, for it has no sun. A major cosmic event knocked the planet off its orbit eons ago and sent it on an elliptic course through the Magnus Star Cluster. Not that this is an unusual event in galactic terms. However, it *is* unusual that life still thrives on this planet despite being orphaned from its sun."

Thapu and Olivia rolled their eyes at each other. Karal rolled eight of them at once.

"Gallivanto's atmosphere is so dense that it retains its core heat, thereby ensuring the existence of liquid water on its surface. And it has lots of water—so much of it that the whole planet is covered in a thick layer that teems with life. Bioluminescent algae thrive there, making the oceans shine in beautiful hues of turquoise and green. People sometimes refer to the planet as the *Wandering Wonder*.

"Gallivanto has picked up several space rocks as it travels in a loop within the Magnus Star Cluster. These stray moons are called Uno, Duo, Trio, and so on. And because of Gallivanto's general central location within the Cluster, the Interstellar Alliance decided to give it one extra moon: Exhibitus."

Only now, Exhibitus lies in shambles not far from here. Thapu shuddered.

"Follow me, please," the service droid said, interrupting the teacher's lecture. The droid gestured towards half-a-dozen empty chairs at the end of the big, oval table.

Thapu hurried after Ms. PT-A as they nervously made their way through the high-ranking Alliance governors, ambassadors, and military beings. The adults gathered in small groups, arguing loudly, blaming each other for the destroyed moon and the stolen Exostar, but Thapu noted that some delegates seemed as lost as they were.

"Stellar coffee?" A robot waiter asked an elegant woman from Plethora as Thapu walked passed them.

The attendee was about to answer when unexpectedly, she flung one hand to her mouth, grasped her stomach with the other, then bolted through the swinging doors, retching along the way. Thapu stared after her in bewilderment.

Unfazed, the robot waiter turned and continued toward the following guests: two A'hmuns who chatted behind their hands.

"Is that the new Ambassador from Plethora?" Thapu heard the first one ask as he glanced at the swinging doors.

"Well, of course, it is," the other snorted.

"Same thing happened to the previous one. When will Plethora ever learn to send space-faring delegates?"

"Ah," the first one said, waving his hand dismissively. "You know very well that Plethorans will always be greenfoots. They will never get their space legs. Digging around in the dirt and planting seeds is all they're good at."

"Suits me fine," the second one said. "Let them dig all they want, as long as it's far away from me."

They both chuckled, then cleared their throats when they realized that Thapu had overheard every word. Thapu blushed, ashamed by the attitude of his people. A'hmuns and Plethorans lived on neighboring planets of the same star system and were known to crack jokes at each others' expense. *But that doesn't make it right*, Thapu thought.

He sat down quickly, glancing at Karal as the alien took a place beside him, and realized that he hadn't been very kind to him. Thapu had gotten to know Karal a lot more in the past five days, and he knew his friend was as terrified as he was. What would the Alliance ask of them? "This will be over soon, Karal. Don't worry," he whispered to the alien, wondering if he believed his own words.

"This mollusk-infused tea from Gallivanto is quite wonderful, isn't it?" A voice said before Karal could answer. Thapu and Karal leaned forward curiously and found, two seats down, a delegate from Enillon sipping on a steaming cup while addressing his neighbor, who happened to be the Gemelan Ambassador. The poor delegate had probably forgotten that Gemelans didn't eat or drink regular food, which meant that the Ambassador had never tasted mollusk-infused tea in his life.

Typically silent, Gemelans rarely shared their thoughts unless absolutely necessary. As an advanced civilization that had cast aside its physical form, they tended to look down on other species. This Gemelan Ambassador was no different. All he did was give an unintelligible grunt as a reply.

The Enillon delegate realized that Thapu was glancing his way, so he quickly broke into an exaggerated laugh, "Ha, ha, ha, Ambassador! You always have the best jokes. Let me tell you one that we have on Enillon..."

Before he could say another word, the Gemelan Ambassador stood and shut off his visibility shield, vanishing at once to the eyes of the others.

Thapu blinked.

The Enillon delegate blushed, realizing he had been blatantly ignored, and ended up staring morosely down at his cup.

A minute later, near the buffet tables, Thapu caught the Gemelan Ambassador reappearing after a guard scolded him for having shut off his visibility shield—something which remained forbidden on the grounds of Interstellar Alliance facilities.

The robot waiters had almost finished serving tea and coffee when the doors swung open, and a group of important-looking delegates entered the room. Most of them were inhabitants from Civicus-1, -2, and -3.

Thapu straightened in his chair, his pulse quickening in spite of himself. He had never seen Civicans from this close, much less their Governor, Masunto Tursis.

Ms. PT-A interrupted his thoughts. "Civicans, who live in the Fourth Quadrant of the Interstellar Alliance, are currently the leaders of the Interstellar Alliance. In the previous quadrant, it was Enillon. Within fifty years, it will be Gemelo's turn." She explained.

Thapu sank in his chair irritably. *Really? Is she going to do this now?*

"Remember, at school, back home? I presented the Interstellar Alliance like the face of a clock, divided into seven sections—one section for each planet. Gallivanto is the single arm on that clock. Whichever section that arm is pointing at means that the planet within it becomes the head of the Interstellar Alliance. It gives everyone a chance to lead the mighty planetary group. Clever, isn't it?

"For now, that arm is pointing at Civicus. In space terms, this means that Gallivanto is traveling closer to Civicus than any other planets. Within fifty years, though, it will wander into Gemelo's neighborhood."

Her voice lowered to a whisper. "As natural administrators and politicians, Civicus takes its leadership role very seriously. It is not looking forward to handing over the reins of the Alliance to Gemelo when the time comes. Many others, however, can't wait for this to happen, as Civicus is accused of being fraught with corrupt bureaucrats and bankers. But, for now, at least, Civicus remains in charge, which means they also need to deal with the mess that the Interstellar Alliance finds itself in today."

Around them, arguments died, and everyone swiftly took their places, forcing Ms. PT-

A to fall silent.

However, Governor Masunto Tursis remained standing and his first words sent a chill down Thapu's spine.

"Gentlebeings," he began, resting deep-set cat-like eyes on the aliens seated around the table. "There is not a minute to spare. Five days ago, our Alliance was viciously attacked. Exhibitus was destroyed, and many of our companions died." He trailed off.

In the heavy silence that followed, dread settled in Thapu's stomach. It had not occurred to him before, but aside from the famous museum, Exhibitus had also housed the Interstellar Alliance Government Offices, where planetary leaders had worked. And many of those leaders were now dead. No wonder half of the attendees looked lost or chatted about greenfoots and mollusk-infused tea instead of the problems at hand. This was probably their first Alliance meeting, ever, and they had no idea what they were facing.

As if confirming his thoughts, Masunto Tursis continued, "Many of you were appointed only a couple of days ago, taking the place of your lost companions, and the burden that falls on your shoulders is devastating. For today, we gather here on Luna Duo to launch the Critical Alliance

Committee, which is tasked with resolving the pressing issue of the stolen Exostar." He paused, looking at them gravely. "Because, gentlebeings, with the Exostar gone, peace is now at stake."

CHAPTER 12 *Accusations*

Masunto Tursis ordered that Ms. PT-A project the full video feed of the attack since all the other service droids and cameras had been sucked out into the vacuum—something she willingly obliged to.

With every passing minute of the video, Olivia felt smaller and smaller. She cringed at the sight of the frightful thief in its insect-like armor. *What next?* She thought. *Will they tell me to speak, also?* How could she relive such a horrible experience in front of a whole room of alien delegates?

"The diamond belongs to us! The Terra Vault belongs to us!" The thief's voice boomed through the conference room through its skull-like helmet.

The words caused a storm. Exclamations broke out. "The Terra Vault!" people muttered. "The thief mentioned the Terra Vault!"

"How do they know about the Terra Vault?"

"Does that mean the thieves have found the Lost Space Treasure?'

Olivia glanced at Thapu and Karal, surprised that adults would speak of a children's bedtime story.

"Who are these thieves, anyway?"

"It was the Vunkotuneans, of course," the Enillon Ambassador said. He had probably meant it as a private comment for his neighbor, but his voice carried over the others, unchaining angry replies.

"Vunkotune rejects this accusation," the massive robot Ambassador from Vunkotune objected.

The Enillon Ambassador didn't back down. "Excuse me! We can all see it as clear as day. Is that not a Vunkotune spaceship sticking out of Exhibitus?"

"It is, indeed," the Vunkotune Ambassador replied with a neutral robotic tone. "Vunkotune reported the disappearance of this spaceship in the year two-hundred-and-twenty-six a.i.a. of the

Fourth Quadrant. The spaceship and its crew, went missing during an exploratory expedition outside the borders of the Interstellar Alliance."

"An exploratory expedition!" the Enillon Ambassador snorted. "Our records show that this spaceship was lurking on the edge of our borders, spying on us. It is common knowledge that Vunkotune intends to take over Enillon and kick out its A'hmun inhabitants. You already tried—and failed—to do this during the Exostar War!"

"The spaceship was *not* spying on Enillon," the Vunkotune Ambassador objected. "Its task was to find a new planet for my people to live on. We signed the Exostar Peace Treaty, don't forget, swearing never to attack one of our Alliance neighbors. We do not go back on our word. It is common knowledge that our Star—a supergiant—is threatening to explode any day, taking my planet with it. It is in my people's interest to find a new home before that happens."

"Exactly," the Enillon Ambassador muttered. "And your eyes are set on Enillon."

Masunto Tursis jumped in before they could clash further. "You have seen the video. The thief addressed children within the exhibit—A'hmun children, to be precise. I doubt this is a coincidence."

All eyes turned toward Oliva, Karal, and Thapu.

Olivia froze. *What?* Did he really think that creepy insect-thing had been talking to her directly?

Fortunately, Masunto Tursis turned towards the Enillon Ambassador. "Have the A'hmun not discovered anything that would explain this thief's statements? Is there nothing in your history records at the Pazorri University that could shed light on the identity of these crooks?"

<Forget A'hmun history,> a Lluunides delegate jumped in, his blubbery voice translating into the common Alliance tongue within everyone's MT devices. <There is no point in searching for an external culprit. This was an insider job.> His eye-stalks roamed around the room. <It is clear to me that someone in this room is behind the Exostar theft!>

Everyone fell silent. Deep distrust marked everyone's faces as they glanced darkly at each other.

"Don't think you are exempt, Lluunides," the Enillon Ambassador snapped.

The Lluunides delegate blinked. <Exempt? Of course, we are cleared of this theft! You do realize that your civilians are alive thanks to the

heroic deeds of the Lluunides child within the Exostar exhibit, don't you?>

Olivia glanced at Karal, who was producing more gooey substance than usual.

"A decoy!" the Enillon Ambassador retorted. "The child's actions mean nothing. We have uncovered that this child's father is a spy! He and his family moved from Lluunides to Enillon under the guise of a fake scholarship at the Pazorri University."

"A spy?" Thapu burst out, making Olivia jump. His face was red. "Karal is *not* a spy! How dare you!"

"Thapu!" Ms. PT-A warned.

Angry voices broke out, shouting over each other.

"DELEGATES!" Ambassador Masunto Tursis shouted. He waited for the attendees to quiet down before continuing. "Please, gentlebeings, sit down. We must focus on the task at hand. It's no use pointing fingers at each other. The Exostar is gone, and as long as it is gone, there will be distrust. We must work together. We must discover who stole the diamond. Discontent and quarrels are brewing among our citizens. We are on the brink of a new Exostar War. We must avoid the collapse of the Alliance at all costs!"

He stabbed his index finger in the air. "Be warned: if one of you is guilty of stealing the Exostar, you will be banished from this Alliance for all eternity. You will be removed from any commercial activity, association, or assistance. You will be on your own. Think hard. Is that a path you would want for your people?"

Masunto Tursis paused, letting his words sink in. "If you hear of anyone—*anyone*—who holds information about these thieves, about the location of the Exostar or the Lost Space Treasure, they must be tracked down and brought in at once. If anyone, in any way, is found to be withholding information from the Alliance for the sole benefit of their planet, they will be atomized without a court ruling."

He paused again. "Mark my words: no means will be too small, no search too thorough, until the one who can lead us to the Exostar is found."

LEAVE A REVIEW:

If you enjoyed this book, please leave a review in the 'Write a customer review' section:

www.amazon.com/dp/B0BKFXY87S

THE ADVENTURE CONTINUES:

EXOSTAR

(The Lost Space Treasure Series, Book 1)

www.amazon.com/dp/B0BKFYBP4V

The Lost Space Treasure Series

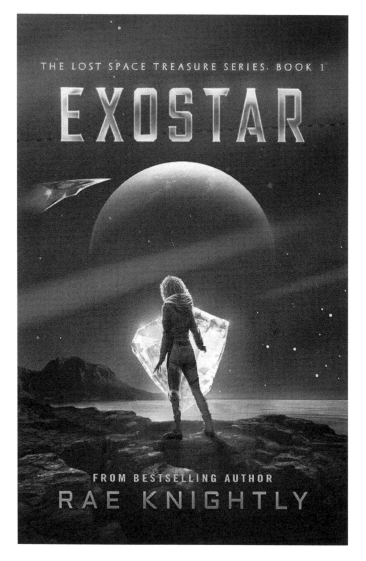

THE LOST SPACE TREASURE SERIES. BOOK 1

EXOSTAR

FROM BESTSELLING AUTHOR
RAE KNIGHTLY

Turn the page and start reading…

K E P R A - 2
INDEPENDENT PLANET
MAGNUS STAR CLUSTER
MILKY WAY GALAXY
INTEREST: NONE.

CHAPTER 1 *The Identity Problem*

Trinket came into existence when she was six years old. There weren't many other ways to put it. One minute, she didn't exist; the next, her eyes flew open, and there she lay on a hard table, the Old Scientist peering down his long nose at her, his thick eyebrows drawn together. It was as if a switch had been activated.

Now, some six years later, she still didn't know who she was or even *what* she was. A *piece of scrap*. That's what the townsfolk called her. *Piece of scrap* was the derogatory name they gave androids that ambled through the streets of

Axiopolis—botched machines created by unscrupulous scientists who messed with robotics and experiments.

Whether she was an android or a mortal being, Trinket guessed that, by now, she was roughly the equivalent of a twelve-year-old girl. But twelve wasn't old enough to fulfill her plan. Twelve was too young to get her off-world.

"Trin Adamton, fourteen years old," she muttered, slightly out of breath as she hobbled up a steep hill towards the Old Scientist's shack. Adamton was a common family name in Axiopolis. She might get away with it.

"Trin Modino, thirteen years old," she tried. Loose pebbles rolled under her right foot, and she fell face-first. Fortunately, her outstretched hands took most of the blow. She caught her breath and rolled on to her back. "For once, my prosthetic leg didn't slip off," she muttered.

Oblivious to her situation, a male voice spoke in her ear. "Please repeat. I didn't hear that."

"You weren't meant to," Trinket mumbled, picking herself up with care so that her prosthetic leg would remain firmly attached to her upper leg stump. She wiped her fingerless gloves together to remove the ochre-colored dust that clung to them, then checked that her Mass Transfer device was still tightly wrapped behind her ear. She couldn't afford to lose it. It was an old-fashioned adult model that didn't have the malleable option to adapt to the wearer's ear, so it was a bit too big for her.

"Please repeat," the device said again.

"Give me a break, Empty," she grunted, plowing forward in spite of the heat. At first, the name Empty had been a bit of a joke. Trinket had found the Mass Transfer device in a junk pile after it had no doubt been cast away in favor of a more modern version. Or perhaps the previous owner— most likely on the run from the Interstellar Alliance Law Enforcement—had wanted to get rid of the last thing tying them to their identity.

People called these mini information computers MTs, for short. Trinket hadn't expected this old model to contain much information, so she had nicknamed it EMpTy.

Only, over the years, Empty had become the closest thing she had had to a friend, and the name had become more than just a silly word. She knew it was just a fancy computer devoid of feelings, but the fact that it didn't have personality modes like the newer models, suited her. Empty never got angry, never judged her, and was always there when she needed it.

"The shuttle to Kepra-1 leaves Space Central in sixty-three-point-two local planetary hours. You must input your final identification details into my core memory prior to that," Empty said helpfully.

"Thanks for the reminder," Trinket grumbled.

Travelers had to be older than twelve and own an MT device linked to their name before they were allowed off-world without adult supervision. Trinket had cracked Empty's core memory and removed the previous owner's details—something she would never have achieved in a newer device. Now she just had to input a new identity—if only she could decide which one would provide her the safest passage.

As if reminding her of the urgency of her task, a distant roar made the ground rumble under her feet. She gazed at the horizon to her right and watched as the daily shuttle to Kepra-1 left Space Central. It shot up from the ground, its powerful thrusters pushing it through the atmosphere in a wide arc. Kepra-1 was rising to the East, the planet's outline warped by the heat.

Trinket sighed. Two more days and she would be on that Shuttle, heading for a better life. It was the only way she could save her prosthetic leg—and the little orphan boy.

She just needed to pick up one last thing from the Old Scientist's home.

She glanced up the hill and figured she had another ten minutes' climb before she reached the rundown shack. *Might as well make the most of it.* "All right, Empty. Give it your best shot." She grimaced, resuming her climb and trying to ignore the tiny but persistent creaking sound of the rusting screw in her metal leg. *Don't you dare snap on me now!*

"Very well," Empty said, breaking through her thoughts. "State your name."

"Trin Adamton," Trinket said at once, welcoming the diversion from her worrisome leg. It was best to avoid the name *Modino*, which was the name of a local mobster family. It could get her into trouble. "Adamton, Adamton," she repeated so that she wouldn't forget.

"State your age."

"Fou… Oh, quarks! Thirteen." She was taller than most children her age, but fourteen was probably stretching it a bit, and could lead to questions.

"State your city and planet of residency."

"Axiopolis. Kepra-2."

"State your city and planet of destination."

"Omopolis. Kepra-1."

"What is the nature of your visit to Omopolis?"

Trinket had to think about that one. "Great question, Empty!" she praised the device.

"Thank you, Trin. What is the nature of your visit to Omopolis?"

Trinket grinned. Empty was playing the part of Shuttle Security very well. She hesitated for a second and blurted out the first thing that came to mind. "I have been sent to Omopolis to buy clothing and medical supplies for the orphans of Axiopolis," she said, then caught herself.

What am I doing, using the orphans like that? She was about to abandon them. Who would shield them from Stinge, their caretaker? Who would keep them out of the mines? Who would tell them bedtime stories? But still—

"Remnant military spacecraft approaching," Empty said in her ear.

—it didn't feel right. She had just used the orphans to get a past Shuttle Securit— "Hold it! *WHAT?*"

Empty repeated patiently, "Remnant military spacecraft approaching. It is coming in from a south-easterly direction. Estimated flyover time: ten seconds."

Trinket reeled. *A Remnant aircraft? Here?*

She glanced around hastily. The hillside was dry and sun-beaten, except for some distant boulders and, not too far off, a single dead tree. Heart thumping, she leaped toward it and plunged into its shadow. As she did so, her prosthetic leg twisted from under her, and she landed hard on her side. "Ouch!" She bit her lip and hastily pulled in the carbon fiber leg that had fallen off her upper left thigh.

Just in time.

A dark cylindrical spacecraft emerged from over the southeastern mountains, lifting a trail of dust as it swooped past her and disappeared behind the top of the hill she had been trying to reach.

Trinket coughed into the end of her scarf headband, blinking against the swirling particles. "The Remnants!" she gasped. "What are they doing here?"

"I don't know the answer to that question," Empty stated. "But that's a Class 1 Remnant spacecraft. The only Class 1 Remnant spacecraft on Kepra-2 belongs to—"

"—Count Solomon Drakir!" she finished, going cold inside. "That can't be good." What could possibly have attracted these cruel invaders to Babbo's home?

She fumbled with her leg. Under normal circumstances, putting it on was a bit of a challenge, but now, nervousness at the Remnant's proximity only made things harder.

"Four steps to walking, four steps to walking," she repeated to calm herself. She had gotten into the habit of saying the steps out loud every time she had to put on her prosthetic leg. It forced her to concentrate, as she had learned the hard way that rushing things could cause it to detach. Taking unwise leaps and sweating from the climb had made it easy for the prothetic leg slip off.

"Step one: the silicone liner." There was a thin layer of red dust on the bare skin of her leg stump. She wiped it away as best she could with the back of her sleeve before pulling up the liner over the stump.

"Step two: the screw." Once the liner fit over her stump like a tight sock, she checked the rusty screw. "Don't you dare give up on me now," she scolded, stabbing a finger at it in a warning.

"Step three: the socket." She slipped her stump into the hard carbon fiber socket of her prosthetic leg, making sure it fit snuggly.

"Step four: remove air." She activated a little

pump at the bottom of the socket, which sucked out the compressed air trapped inside. This welded her stump tightly into the metal leg, ensuring that the latter wouldn't rotate while she walked.

"There," she finished, staring at her only means of mobility. She tapped the metal leg as if reassuring an old friend and nodded to herself. "Babbo did a good job. It'll hold; I know it will."

She knew her inorganic leg as well as she did the back of her organic-looking hand. She knew its weaknesses and how close the screws were to snapping in half from so many years of use. It was high time she found a replacement—and that could only happen on Kepra-1.

She glanced up the remainder of the hill and made her way up again. "Let's find out what the Remnants are doing in my house, Empty," she said.

"That is no longer your house, Trin. And proceeding is not recommended," Empty advised. "The probability that you will get caught by the Remnants is high. And the probability that they will kill you is even higher."

"Right," Trinket agreed, reaching the top and peeking cautiously over the ledge. She gritted her teeth. "And when did that ever stop me?"

CONTINUE READING:
EXOSTAR
(The Lost Space treasure Series, Book 1)
www.amazon.com/dp/B0BKFYBP4V

FREE RESOURCES AND SPACE MAP :
www.raeknightly.com

FREE NOVELLA:
The Great War of the Kins:
www.raeknightly.com

About the Author

Rae Knightly is a bestselling, award-winning author who invites the young reader on a journey into the imagination, where science fiction and fantasy blend into the real world. Young heroes are taken on gripping adventures full of discovery and story twists.

Rae Knightly lives in Vancouver with her husband and two children. She is the winner of the 2022 Whistler Independent Book Awards—Children's Category.

Follow Rae Knightly on social media:
Facebook/Instagram/Twitter/Pinterest
E-mail: raeknightly@gmail.com

Acknowledgments

Special thanks to author Cristy Watson
for helping me untie the plot-knots in
The Lost Space Treasure Series.

The Lost Space Treasure Series is a team effort. As
a self-published author, I could not have produced
a quality story without the help of a professional
book cover designer (thank you, Roger Despi),
beta readers, ARC-readers, and a supportive
writing community.

And finally, a special thank you to you, reader,
for taking the time to read
THE LOST SPACE TREASURE—A NOVELLA.

Thank you!
Rae Knightly

Made in the USA
Columbia, SC
19 November 2023

26738446R00067